MY RACE IS NOT YOURS TO WIN

RAIN OVER TORMENTED MINDS MAY MAKE A MILLION THINK

DANISH ALTAF BAKSHI

Contents

FOREWORD

I always wondered what does it take to express freely without any consciousness.

Is it the capability of introspecting ?

Is it being a torchbearer of a silent revolt ?

For me, it is just being courageous enough to think and express.

When I read Danish's manuscript, I was stunned to find someone whose thoughts were fearlessly different and same as fine. The similarities in our work are surprising. While I went through this Magnum Opus, I came to a vivid conclusion that this work, however distinct in terms of views, has no scope for any opprobrium.

He has written down every aspect of being a black skeep that we both are. Along with our lively conjunctions of reality, this book has also made our association flawless being related to the perceptions.

His thoughts are beyond limits and can be conceptualised by any sane mind.

It is not just his story, it is my story too, it is your story as well.

It is everyone's story. But, the only difference being that some of us are capable of putting it down on paper whilst others struggle with the inability to do so.

I wish him all the success with this artwork of perfection. His mind is capable of turning the world upside down, which you will realise as you read this book.

> *"Wars are not just won by a mere focus on physical strength, but by mental applications first."*

Yours only,
Bhavna Dahiya
Author of 'Your Perception is not my Reality'

Preface

"“Wake up to reality!

Nothing ever goes as planned in this accursed world. The longer you live, the more you realize that the only things that truly exist in this reality are merely pain. suffering and futility.

Everywhere you look in this world, wherever there is light, there will always be shadows to be found as well. As long as there is a concept of victors, the vanquished will also exist. The selfish intent of wanting to preserve peace initiates war. and hatred is born in order to protect love.

There are nexuses causal relationships that cannot be separated.

I want to sever the faith of this world; a world of only victors; a world of only peace; a world of only love; I will create such a world.

~ The Ghost of Uchiha ~"

Prologue

> *"Who you are authentically is alright"*

'No matter what your differences are, you have to embrace them and be proud of the way you are.'

Stop apologizing for existing !

It's ok if your ideas are different, your goals are big - don't be afraid of what others would say. You are skilled, capable, talented - you deserve to be a leader, and you are enough.

> *"Leaning in can be uncomfortable, so don't be afraid to own your seat, lean back, and kick your feet up." - Joy Fitzgerald*

Writing a book always seemed too daunting a task to me; it was as if collecting words at a single page is a no-brainer.

But then, I wrote this book. Am I writer in that case ?

If it means caging me into a category of a conventional writer, then I'm not. I am just a human trying to put his thoughts into words.

Sometimes, being different feels a lot like being alone. But with that being said, being true to that and being true to my standards and my way of doing things, everything that has made me feel very different; in the end, it has made me the happiest of all.

So, here is this book conveying my thoughts to you all. The thoughts that are uniquely unfitting in this society but, are thoughts worthy of being shared.

I

The Social Upheaval of an Epoch

Clutching my soul, I stood on the styx;
hankering for liberation, my silhouette stretched.
Reminiscing; I, finally, set myself free

ꟻ

I was red, they coloured me green;
wings clipped, I slithered.
Little did they realise, passion shepherded the cosmos.

ꟻ

As I invaded you, the bewitching eyes dominated me;
defloration established my monopoly.

Immortality we attained; became pyromaniacs.

ꕥ

Counting the stars, I tried to forget the moon;
but fate screamed.
You thwacked me with destiny; even Ares could not outdo me

ꕥ

Fire for them, warmth for you;
dominance to submission, I undertook pilgrimage.
Redemption or damnation, the world questioned.

I tried to bribe the reality;
but even Janus could not anticipate.
Desolated, I stood anxious for the dinkum oil, ultimately leading to my own devastation

The obverse was plutonium and the reverse was platinum.
Existed cheek by jowl, separation attacked the significance;
coalescence could lead to holocaust.
Union or sunder ?
Even they didn't know

Hues of existence revamped me;
nuanced I became, espoused by the bed of roses.

I was the black sheep, duplicitous they countered;
I baptised myself 'fey'.

ഇ

Fiction were my veins, fantasy ran through them;
understood as alike but disparate.
Just like the two worlds I inhabited;
velvet dominated the vale of tears.

ഇ

The aeon of impersonators it is, even the queen of the garden conceals prickles.

One city with slums and schloss, shivoo and shiva, prosperous and penurious;

married but divorced.

II

The Enchanted Intensity

While crossing the Chinvat bridge, I finally had nothing to hide;

throwing off the weight from my shoulders, I unravelled the mystery of conduct.

I assimilated the surmise of silence -
Reticence to Remain.

Walking down the aisle of affliction, I wept tears of fatigue.
Facing the east I stood, the dawn of candour derided me;
At least I managed to pretend that the fire was extinguished.

They gifted me a clock, persuasion played its way;
naive I was, chased them.
Realisation took time, but time only led to the moment of death.

They called me 'She of the west' as I welcomed the Gordian knot;
it fed on my own blood by degrees.
Deeper I dug, enigmatic I became;
conundra led the way, I went astray.

&

They built a wall so that I could not attain peace;
had they known he was my horcrux maybe the efforts might have ceased.
Lacerated my soul, I resorted to silence, tranquillity or impending disaster;
I counted on Alzheimer's, at least embraced that vizard.

&

Dazzles of existence enclosed as confidential,
I chased with a yearning to disclose.
A shadow couldn't help, I tried, had to exchange vows with fate;
if only I had the key to disclose,
but had the deal off the table forever.

&

Velvet linen, stupendous charm,

an astronomical choice of comforts,
a titanic dynasty and neverending attention;
not an iota of doubt about a state of plenty and worth.
But, dreamt of a camouflaged survival,
in the lap of intense love with a shrilling touch of solace;
suspired, never slept satiated.

ᘓ

It's just another night and I'm staring at the moon as my eyes brighten up to see the way I have led into the race.
I came a long way past heartbreaks and hardships standing high but without a heart pounding inside.
The voice got crushed beneath the curses of the struggle ahead of which I bled my way.
I can see the stars who exemplify the infinite tears to pace up.
The cliff I owned, crowned me the queen;
reigning over none but the reality,
I faced an identity crisis or was it a crisis of resilience I drowned myself in the ocean of perilous existence.

ᘓ

Can you catch me when I slip ?
Can you paint me when i black out ?
Can you help me get sober when I get drugged with troubles ?
Can you be the answer to my unanswered questions ?
Can you just be you ?
I undertook a journey where I found the lost me and grew suspicious of even the virtuous.

The world didn't catch me but could have let me down gradually.

The world coloured my life grey by mixing the shrouded intentions with your real motive of blacking me out.

The world overdosed me with your Judas kiss.

The world forever locked me up in the prison of mysteries.

But, I was never a maybe.

ꕤ

Head held high,
destiny arrested,
embracing the robe of honour,
I was the Cleopatra of my Egypt.
The crown jewelled with gems of affliction,
The strong woman was still naive inside.
It's crazy how circumstances stab.

ꕤ

III

The Paradox of Expression

Enter Caption

Standing as guards at the prison, fragile but protected.

As light crept its way through them, my morning woke me up.

Brown or white or any other, they lit my den.

Shut me from the outside race, helped me to conceal my limits, they always were there no matter what.

I grew up seeing those jewellery on my home's body.

In each corner they stood, in solidarity, just standing like scarecrows;

just standing but shielding.

Although they have replacements, I would never replace them because they stood by me when others tried to replace me.

But we only miss them when it's bright even if they are honest during dark days.

We only know they matter when we forget to shut them up.

Even though lifeless, they are my guardians when the sun hits hard.

They open the window of gaiety when heaven cries tears of rain.

They clutch me in their lap and sing to me, just like a mother does, when I wish to escape from the outerly.

They saw me grow up, cry, laugh, hide, confused, hopeless, energetic and saw me give up and again stand up to fight with a sharper sword this time.

Now that I have to leave all this behind, I weep and look for a reason to stay.

Who knew materialistic things could personify.

Well, for the world they were just curtains on a wall, dead, just adding to the beauty of a room;

but, for me, they were full of life,

a silent onlooker who became so important to me that i missed them in my new palace such that i never put on curtains in the glass house again.

ꟺ

Optimism and pessimism,
though,
are two different worlds but interconnected.
Optimism is being free from pessimism but pessimism takes hold only if you get too optimistic.
You behold tears and pretend but it's not too late;
you camouflage the reality but it was never yours.
Diametrically opposite are the voices in my brain,
but my heart jumps up and consoles me.
I've been searching for a trail of fire to ignite the secrets.
Clipped wings lead to suicide but even Maleficent learnt to live.
If you don't part from the nest, the sky would never be yours.

ꟺ

The hands on the waist and eyes narrating the story,
She overtook the world.
Ruling hearts, the Queen was enough.
But the sleepless nights,
injured spirit,
and the glass house seemed ironic of the crown she adorned.

ꕥ

You were the iron to my furnace,
the thunder in my rains.
You burnt yourself to give me meaning,
I shook every time as you lightened up.

ꕥ

Love emanated from within,
meaningless though in a world governed by musketeers.
Easily pulled off the ethical being,
The theory of karma was killed and buried deep.

ꕥ

Running to a new refuge,
we were wasted and lost,
but we found our home in each other.
Laying under the stars,
We found the keys to the lock of universal freedom.
Although we were assassinated,
we became immortal.
Lived the vows of living and dying together.

ꕥ

You are my star,
so far but so close;
awestruck,
I just keep staring but never embrace a touch.
They say that the thing we love the most is a deterrent,
But what's an adventure without a roller coaster or a life without risk?

ꝏ

I spilled ink on my paper,
just to make it colourful.
Trying to go beyond the league,
I,
rather,
became the rule breaker.
No one cared about,
'It's your canvas, paint it the way you want'.

ꝏ

The Night of brightness brought about the dawn of despair.
The tears of patience,
smiles to hide the pain of waiting and the anxious look at the door.
Seeing him leaving,
I wanted to go along wherever he could take me,
but when you're drowning,
it's better not to take another along with you down.

IV

The Insanity of Existence

Just like how the first cry of a baby soothes a mother's soul,
The lyrics of forgiveness did mine.
Quarrelled and screamed but inside the water,
no one heard.
All it took was one 'apology' for always taking myself granted always,
but apologies are also often taken for granted.

ꕥ

Criticised as hedonist, never over self interest;
the Lokyata ethics in me smiled off.
Selfish ?
No !
Just surviving.
Had it been selfish,
Krishna would have never loved his Radha.

ꕤ

Rage on its peak,
villainized goodness,
terror to behold,
always the 'bad';
but somewhere the heart was longing to be unlocked.
Elena also transformed Damon Salvatore;
conquering the odds,
exemplified true love.

ꕤ

Did it ever feel that,
however loud you scream,

at last the voice is only heard by the empty paper,
waiting for you to pour down your feelings?
Just like you're under the ocean and nothing really helps;
but you still don't give up searching for a plank to float upon.

ꕤ

You came into my life just like a moonbow.
Just as it needs a full moon night to be spotted,
so did I need the perfect situation to have you.
Just as it is found mostly amidst mist,
so did I find you mostly in my vulnerable situations.

Having wasted months before exams with the determination of starting the preparation the next day,
I sighed on the night just before the exam thinking:
'If I only got one more day.....'
Nothing has changed even now, it's all the same,
just the concern is different.
'If only I got one more shot at childhood.'

'All good boys go to heaven, but bad boys bring heaven to you'.

Thank you Julia Michaels for telling us that -

Sometimes, we all need to put our guards back up and be bad and own it,

to find our own 'heaven'.

Because,

accepting the 'bad' me is better than fighting with the 'good' image of me.

ꕤ

Diving off the highest cliff;

Camping at the peak,

screaming in the highest pitch,

surviving yet another day,

I chose to believe that I conquered all the odds.

Yet,

the fear of returning home which was no longer a 'home' with memories but my people,

always grew as rapidly as a forest fire,

burning everything in its way.

ꕤ

Hate is stronger than love.

Have you ever thought why hating Klaus Mikaelson was easier than loving Stefan Salvatore ?

No one cared about how he served his life on a platter for his love,

We all cared about the 'evident' love of the Salvatore brothers.

ꕤ

Fears of agony disappeared,
all doubts vanished and we were freed from all prisons.
That was the moment when our eyes lit fireworks and the balance of life was restored.

V

Causation of Rebellions

I tried to imagine the reactions to my actions.

The nightmare came as a blessing in disguise which opened up all the locks.

ꕤ

How can we imagine what cannot exist ?

It's just like counting on the moon in a lunar eclipse and ignoring all the stars on a normal night.

ꕤ

Asking constantly for flowers,
spring swiftly answered,
'Every breeze who once walked along, left'.
Asking constantly for flowers, thorns answered,
'I forever stuck by, but was despised'.

Colour me in your colour,
to colour the world around,
in different colours.
I don't care about the 'Blacks and whites',
They are even found in people.

While I was busy finding shelter,
The seasons left me alone.
When I started noticing the seasons,
I forgot my way home.

The soul rose high,
waving at the body and searching for another to give meaning to life.
The theory was reversed here;
sometimes,
Separation is inevitably beautiful.

Still holding onto the last hope;
even the moon dresses up differently everyday,
What are humans?
Still holding onto the last hope;
I sailed through just like Noah did,
and didn't have to listen to them.

Time is always like Brutus ,
but stars are aligned.
The perfect intensity with which destiny thwacked us,
we will defy the norms of patience.

Intentions with which you came in,
burnt down the glaciers of doubt.
However wrong they were,
I found the needle in the heap.

I want to steal the good in the Devil.
Angels are not capable of wrong.
But,
What is better ?
The ray of light in darkness or no scope of a different sky altogether ?

VI

Chaos and Moonlight

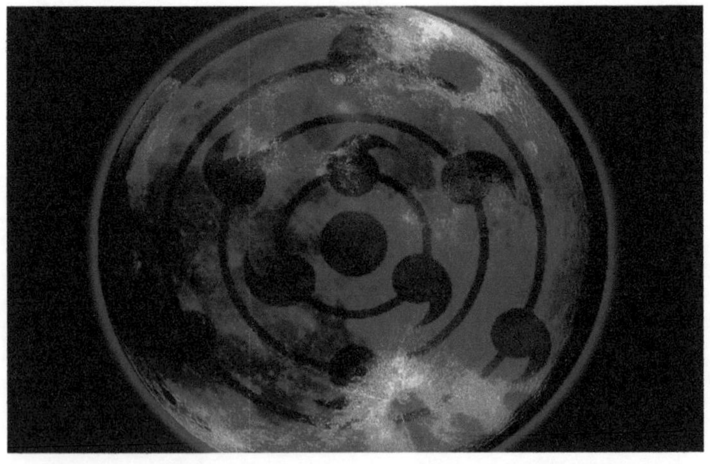

Enter Caption

Where do you think you're going ?

I questioned myself.
It's not always the road that you need to walk on,
but the perfect shoes to fit in to keep you going,
I answered my conscience.

ஐ

It won't be too long now before I catch those netted rays penetrating through the hopeful panes.
I wonder,
Is it ever too late ?

ஐ

One, two, three;
slowly,
Everyone started falling.
'It's negligible',
said the flower.
The petals questioned it in autumn,
'Is it still negligible ?'.

ஐ

I had no regrets,
It was magic.
Turning down the life I adorned,
I gifted myself anew.
I still remember the moment;

It was magic.

Conceal to heal;
stitching together the hard lines of reality,
it made me wonder,
'Why do I hide to satisfy myself ?
So that they may conform to my life ?

There will come a day when water will turn red,
the sky will turn black and constellations will no longer pave the way;
the day when destiny starts rewriting itself.

I found the cure for the diagnosis which is yet unknown.
Kept smiling;
precautions are sometimes wonderful.

It seems like I lose myself all over again.
Who am I ?
Just a product of what they created ?
My soul stands corrupt and I can't even look me in the eye.
Fulfilling all the expectations,
I cry out loud but no one hears me.
Sacrifices are hell bent on crushing me all over every time.
What's my worth ?
Listening to those voices screaming, my demons inside are incapable of lifting me anymore. For once, I wanna vanish and create the vacuum that I used to fill.
Nothing ever could bring me back because I'll be gone then.
No more promises to be broken,
no more expectations to be catered to,
no more labels to carry;
for once I will be liberated.
Exemplifying faithfulness isn't for me,
for no one can be worth letting me down.

ꙮ

'I believe in vicarious love',
said my heart to flowers who are loved by the sun.
The knot also tied me up with the fictional me that was alive on paper.

ꙮ

When black power met the red passion,
a resilient brown was born.
Embracing the ability to withstand disasters,
the souls grew closer and emitted the potential of precognition.

ꕤ

The Forgotten Acquaintance

In the corner of the dilapidated classroom sat an even more dilapidated desk. like an old monk it meditated near the window, observing the ever expanding universe.

as the netted sun rays filtered through the pane. they ascended the sketches and doodles. The desk bore the markings like some sacred pattern from the red Indian tribe.

for us it was merely a desk; nothing more, nothing less. we would

come each day, and adumbrate the wood.

some would doodle on it, others would spill ink on it, but regardless of what you did, it created an everlasting mark.

what might have started as a small drawing a year ago, had by the end of the year grown into a full canvas.

a caricature drawn in the middle, a formula etched on the side. it was an amalgamation of varying thoughts. spirals ran across

the borders, and the artistry of the whitener was displayed proudly at the corners.

a drawing of shinchan adorned the left corner, and Einstein's equation lay diagonally across from it. little did we realise that this panorama of a seat had been home to so many of us.

It has accommodated a future astronaut, a painter, an activist and a throng of diverse and unique individuals bound to change the world.

it has seated the pass-out and would seat the next batch too.

It has doubled as an exam desk and a stepping stool for board work.

it has become a stage when there was no teacher around and had served as the detect bunker for mid-class snacks. It was our trusted old man.

and like the faithful acquaintance it was, it would hear all our secrets and bury them in its splinters and dentures. Now, on the last day of our school, we stare at the desk, teary-eyed. no one

could have ever imagined that a carved piece of wood could be such an integral part of our journey.

it was the desk, into which we whispered secrets, and cried silently. The seat had been an auditor and a counsellor. and without our notice it has immortalised our school experience. and of all things, i believe, i would miss this old and antiquated canvas the most.

VII

The Questions that remained Unanswered

Enter Caption

It was just another hectic day and I was running short on time. I was already five minutes late and covering 500 metres in another five minutes seemed next to impossible. My heart was pumping so fast that I felt as if it would jump out any second. It happened to be my same routine as daily but something about the day was very different . My stress was displaced by ease and I felt no hurry. I felt as if the clock had stopped just for me, to honour me or to celebrate with me ,I did not know. Whether some miracle was going to happen or was it a sign of a bad omen, it was unpredictable. It was a normal autumn morning for everybody but for me.

I even loved those leaves sleeping on the road and others waiting for their turn to get free. Unlike other mornings when they irritated me, that day I wanted to dance to the rhythm of the chirpings of little birds and sing along the sprinting leaves. Something was different about the day. While walking in my world of fantasy, my attention diverted to the lovely rose fragrance that came from behind me.

As I turned back, I saw a tall, beautiful, perfectly shaped lady in the morning stage of her life, dressed in an elegant wine dress. Her blonde locks were neatly tied up which further enhanced her sharp features. She looked extremely stunning that I kept looking at her without blinking as she passed by me. Her sunglasses hid her eyes as she walked the street with her abnormally high heels. Whether she did not notice me or she chose to ignore me, I do not know. She was perhaps the most beautiful female I had ever seen in my life.

While all of this happened, my eyes suddenly rested on the clock which displayed sharp 10:00AM, which simply put, means that I was late, really late. I had to reach the office by 9:30AM sharp and I was literally half an hour late already.

I was sure I would be fired.

But, on reaching the office, I was intimated that my boss was absent on account of high fever. A person who never missed a chance to shout at his employees for being late was absent. Quite strange to digest, but I had to.

This went on till days; I noticed that lady passing by the same road daily. This made me wonder whether she was blind that she failed to notice me or was she just minding her own business.

One day, I was just clicking some pictures on the road. Although I do not consider myself a good photographer to capture the essence of the object captured, but, whenever I take up the camera, it feels as if I am the only one capable of clicking. So, while I was at my endeavours, she passed by me and got accidentally captured in my camera.

It was a sunday morning and the sun was on its high that day. Passing by me daily, I was really curious to know who she really was.

Why did she just start using this road in the last two weeks ?

Was she new in town ?

I followed her without her noticing me. I kept on following her and walked past some unknown streets which were insanely quiet. I, put simply, was spying on her. I followed her for about 20 minutes and then stood still at a place that I had never seen before.

A deep pallor spread around me and everything was just so depressing there. Behind two oak trees, I saw a multi-storeyed house; probably an abandoned one, hiding behind those two guards.

Sky turned red and an ominous silence enveloped me.

I saw her sliding the door and entering that house. She turned back to ensure that no one followed her. Although no one did according to her, I did. I kept hiding behind the wall that bordered the house. As soon as she entered, I stood up and started stepping towards the gate. It seems that no one wanted me to enter that house, which was evident from the gusty wind which was blowing in an opposite direction pushing me away and the grass which clasped onto me as if telling me to stay there and not to enter that house. But, I did.

To my great surprise, as soon as I entered the house, I saw a decent, antique set up inside the house. It was so well maintained that I was so amazed to see it. It was probably the houses which one dreams of. Huge portraits hung on walls signified creativity and an artistic approach. Although the furniture seemed of the nineties but was very well maintained and was a mark of authenticity. This was the image that I captured standing at the door.

As I stepped in, my feet turned cold and I felt a bit unusual. When I entered, a bleak sound emerged from the staircase side which was probably of a lady.

'So, you finally accompanied me till here. Were you spying on me ?'.

I felt as if my world slipped below my feet. I was scared and my heart ran very fast. I had no words to say to her.

My eyes rested on her and I was scared.

Just like a prisoner of war caught up by the enemy authorities. I had no words to say and even my brain did not have an answer to it as well. Finally, some words slipped through my tongue.

No, actually I saw the door open so I.... I... I,,,,,,,,,,

'So, you just entered ?'

I took some steps backwards slightly as she approached me.

She, out of a great surprise, said, 'Would you like to have a coffee with me ?.'

I did not answer and she assumed it was a yes and asked me to sit on the couch when she went into the kitchen to get us coffee. We both sat on the couch, sipping coffee. I did not utter a single word. I did not want to either.

She broke the silence by narrating a story.

'I was just a kid of eleven, when I shifted to London with my aunt and left this place. Although I was too young to attach to a place, I felt secure and peaceful here. I never wanted to leave, but circumstances made me. Adverse times give you the courage to do whatever you do not want to, you see. My mom and dad died in a car accident when I was five and my aunt brought me up. She decided to leave this place forever as it revived unpleasant memories every second that we spent here. So, it has been twenty years now and I still miss this place.'

I heard about it like a girl of five hears a fairytale. So, why did she return now; this question kept bugging my mind but I did not have the courage to ask her.

'So, you must be wondering why have I returned now after all these years ?.'

Was she a mind reader ? I wondered as I was so shocked on hearing this.

I nodded my head in great surprise.

'I returned here as I plan to renovate this house and sell it off.' she sighed.

' I also came here to meet my old friend, who used to be my soulmate till I lived here. We used to eat, play, study, sleep, laugh, cry; everything together.

So, where does she live ?, I asked.

'Oh I am sorry, I forgot to mention, that I will have to meet her in the cemetery, her home; she died. She died the next day I left this place. I was not able to come here even during her funeral. She was burnt alive in her house as the home caught fire due to a leak in the cylinder. I have even heard that no one has ever returned from the house where she breathed her last breath.'

She told me as tears rolled down her cheeks. I realised that coffee had finished when I took my last sip.

'But, it is still a mystery how the house caught fire and she died." She lost her parents too as soon as she was born and was brought up by a nanny. She was the little owner of her parents' wealth that was left behind . Her anny always took care of her, but aspired to be the sole owner of the house out of her greed. I came here to know how my friend really died as I doubt other rumours. I came here to seek revenge for her death.'

She started laughing in a curious way very loudly. This freaked the hell out of me. I felt so dumbstruck that I felt paralysed, unable to move. Her voice echoed in her bungalow. But, I gathered courage and ran out of the house in a matter of seconds.

This unexpected meet with with a stranger left a profound impact on me, making me xenophobic.

I went to the office the next day, even if I did not want to and out of a great surprise, I did not find that lady that day. After reaching the office, everyone looked at me as if trying to sympathise or maybe a look that a criminal gets.

My colleague ran towards me and asked worriedly, 'Are you alright ? How are you feeling now ?.

This question sent me into a state of confusion.

But, what happened ?

Her reply shocked me even further.

She said that she found me unconscious outside the 'Hickens Villa' - an abandoned house for years. She further said that I was found there by a stranger who luckily took me to a nearby hospital and then she took me home. I had no words to express my feelings.

I just said, 'Oh yes ! Ummm thanks, I... I am fine now.'

Who was she who narrated that story ?

Why did she disappear ?

These questions which were unanswered, intrigued me and made me visit the house again.

I saw it locked.

Gazing at the house as the sun dropped the horizon, a passerby came and asked me,

'What happened dear ? Were you another victim ?

You are not shocked when you get surprises one after the other. I experienced it.

She told me that the owner, brought up by her nanny, was burnt alive in the house. Unluckily, the girl claseted onto her nanny, causing the death of the duo. It is believed that she still inhabits the place but from a parallel universe. The house was abandoned and red taped after the accident. This remark further surprised me.

Until I made sense of what she said, I realised that she hooked onto something like...?

When the question slipped through my tongue, I couldn't see her around. She probably left.

This question remains unanswered even today.

Why did that owner tell me her story? Was it just hallucinations or an intentionally occurred incident? Why did that lady label me as a victim?

But as a rule, life moves on and so did I. Work continued just as before and the stress made me overcome those unanswered questions. Even still I do visit that place sometimes, probably once in two weeks, to ponder upon that incident or probably to lie to myself every time that I won't be visiting here again.

GLOSSARY

Chapter 1

Styx -

In Greek mythology, Styx is a deity and a river that forms the boundary between Earth (Gaia) and the Underworld

Pyromaniacs -

Pyromania is a type of impulse control disorder that is characterized by being unable to resist starting fires.

Ares -

Ares is the Greek god of courage and war. He is one of the Twelve Olympians, and the son of Zeus and Hera.

Janus -

He is the god of beginnings, gates, transitions, time, duality, doorways, passages, frames, and endings. He is usually depicted as having two faces.

Chapter 2

Chinvat Bridge -

The Chinvat Bridge or the Bridge of the Requiter in Zoroastrianism is the sifting bridge, which separates the world of the living from the world of the dead.

Horcrux -

A Horcrux was an object in which a Dark Wizard or Witch had hidden a fragment of his or her soul in order to become immortal.

Cleopatra -

Cleopatra VII Philopator was Queen of the Ptolemaic Kingdom of Egypt from 51 to 30 BC, and its last active ruler. A member of the Ptolemaic dynasty, she was a descendant of its founder Ptolemy I Soter, a Macedonian Greek general and companion of Alexander the Great.

Chapter 3

Karma -

It is the force generated by a person's actions held in Hinduism and Buddhism to perpetuate transmigration and in its ethical consequences to determine the nature of the person's next existence Each individual is born with karma, the residual from past lives that must be resolved

Chapter 4

Hedonism -

the ethical theory that pleasure (in the sense of the satisfaction of desires) is the highest good and proper aim of human life.

Lokyata -

Charvaka, also called Lokayata (Sanskrit: "Worldly Ones"), a philosophical Indian school of materialists who rejected the notion of an afterworld, karma, liberation (moksha), the authority of the sacred scriptures, the Vedas, and the immortality of the self.

Krishna and Radha -

It is believed that Krishna enchants the world, but Radha enchants even him. Therefore, she is the supreme goddess of all and together they are called as Radha-Krishna. In many Vaishnava sections, Radha Krishna are often identified as the avatars of Lakshmi Narayan

Damon and Elena -

Damon Salvatore is a fictional character In L. J. Smith's novel series The Vampire Diaries. At the start of season 1, Damon was a self-proclaimed loner,[8] often keeps to himself. Despite his initially antagonistic relationships with humans such as Alaric Saltzman and Sheriff Elizabeth Forbes, Caroline's mother. Damon gradually involved himself in the lives of many people in Mystic Falls by developing friendships with several humans. After spending time with Elena Gilbert, Damon becomes more empathetic and falls deeply, madly and passionately in love with her. He always puts her safety first before anyone else, even his.

Julia Michaels -

Julia Carin Cavazos, known professionally as Julia Michaels, is an American singer and songwriter. Born in Iowa and raised in California, Michaels began her career writing for other artists.

Klaus Mikaelson -

Niklaus Mikaelson was the main protagonist (and sometimes antagonist/anti-hero) of The Originals. He was a former main character, antagonist/anti-hero of The Vampire Diaries. Klaus was an Original vampire and a werewolf, making him the Original Hybrid.

Chapter 5

Noah -

Noah features as the tenth and last of the pre-Flood patriarchs in the traditions of Abrahamic religions. His story appears in the Hebrew Bible (Book of Genesis, chapters 5–9), the Quran and Baha'i writings. Noah is referenced in various other books of the Bible, including the New Testament, and in associated deuterocanonical books.

Brutus -

Marcus Junius Brutus,, c. 85 BC – 23 October 42 BC), often referred to simply as Brutus, was a Roman politician, orator, and the most famous of the assassins of Julius Caesar.

Expression Is My Dance On Flames, Like A Bonfire

"This was my insanity dressed up in a veil of expression.

The insanity that takes the form of rebellion, a form of a satirical survival."

Expression of my thoughts in this book is just a way of letting you all know about my way, which differs from your way.

"In order to be irreplaceable, one must always be different."

9 798887 33514

Printed by Libri Plureos GmbH in Hamburg,
Germany